MAR 8 2005 DATE DUE			
APR - 7 2005			

Pet Care

A GUINEA PIG FOR YOU

Caring for Your Guinea Pig

Written by Susan Blackaby
Illustrated by Charlene DeLage

Content Advisers: Jennifer Zablotny, D.V.M.
Kerrie Burns, D.V.M.
Reading Adviser: Susan Kesselring, M.A., Literacy Educator
Rosemount-Apple Valley-Eagan (Minnesota) School District

PICTURE WINDOW BOOKS
Minneapolis, Minnesota

Editor: Nadia Higgins
Designer: Nathan Gassman
Page production: Picture Window Books
The illustrations in this book were painted with watercolor.

Picture Window Books
5115 Excelsior Boulevard
Suite 232
Minneapolis, MN   55416
1-877-845-8392
www.picturewindowbooks.com

Printed in the United States of America.
1 2 3 4 5 6 08 07 06 05 04 03

Library of Congress Cataloging-in-Publication Data
Blackaby, Susan.
A guinea pig for you : caring for your guinea pig / written by Susan Blackaby ;
illustrated by Charlene DeLage.
v. cm. — (Pet care)
Contents: What is a guinea pig?—A cage for a guinea pig—Food for a guinea pig— Taking care
of your pet—A happy, healthy guinea pig—Make a pet care idea web—Fun facts—Guide to rodents.
ISBN 1-4048-0119-7 (lib. bdg.)
1. Guinea pigs as pets—Juvenile literature. [1. Guinea pigs as pets.]
1. DeLage, Charlene, 1944– ill. II. Title.
SF459.G9 .B58 2003
636.9'3592—dc21
2002155009

TABLE OF CONTENTS

What Is a Guinea Pig?

A guinea pig is not a pig at all.

A guinea pig is actually a rodent.

It can also be a gentle, furry friend.

Guinea pigs are bigger than hamsters and rats, which are also rodents. Guinea pigs come in lots of colors. They can have long hair or short hair.

A Cage for a Guinea Pig

A guinea pig needs a roomy cage with high sides.

The cage needs to have a solid floor.

It needs a cover if you have other pets.

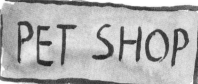

6

The cage needs soft bedding to keep it cozy.

It should be easy to clean.

Bedding

Not Good	cedar shavings
	sawdust
	kitty litter
Good	hardwood shavings
	shredded paper
	corncobs
Better	hay
Best	a mix of hardwood shavings, shredded paper, and hay

The Perfect Place for a Guinea Pig

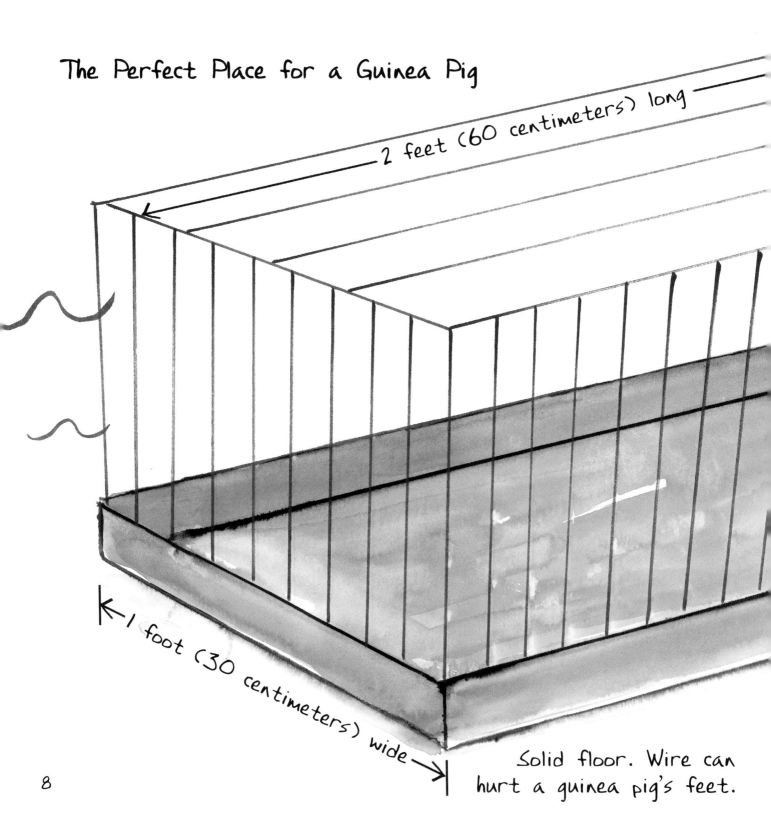

2 feet (60 centimeters) long

1 foot (30 centimeters) wide

Solid floor. Wire can hurt a guinea pig's feet.

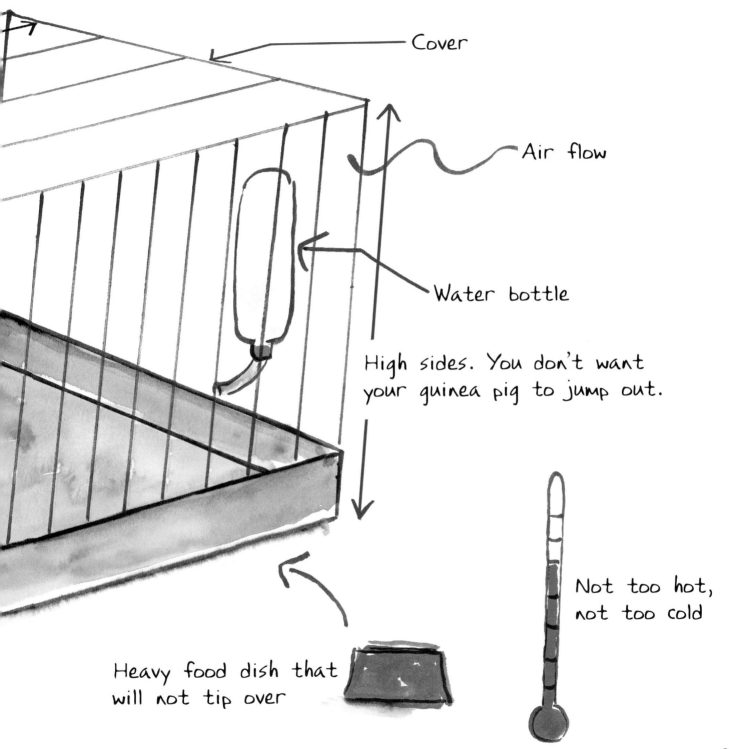

Cover

Air flow

Water bottle

High sides. You don't want
your guinea pig to jump out.

Not too hot,
not too cold

Heavy food dish that
will not tip over

9

A guinea pig needs a place to hide and rest.

A little house will give your guinea pig some peace and quiet.

What makes a good guinea pig house?

- an oatmeal carton

- a shoe box

- a flowerpot

- a wide plastic pipe

Food for a Guinea Pig

A guinea pig eats plants.

It eats food pellets made just for guinea pigs.

The hay in the cage is good for it, too.

Guinea pigs get extra vitamin C
from fresh fruits and vegetables.

GUINEA PIGS LIKE THESE TREATS:

apple slices

carrots

lettuce

broccoli

grapes

orange slices

Do not let your
guinea pig eat
nuts, seeds, or pits.

Taking Care of Your Pet

Taking care of a guinea pig is easy.

Change the bedding in the cage every day.

Scrub the cage floor with soap and water once a week.

14

Change the water every day.

Get rid of old food and wash the dish.

Brush your guinea pig's fur.

Clip your guinea pig's toenails.

Guinea pigs need exercise to stay healthy.

Take your guinea pig outside on warm days.

Set up a pen so that it cannot run away.

Be sure there is plenty of shade and no wind.

A Happy, Healthy Guinea Pig

Healthy guinea pigs are lively. They have bright, shiny eyes.

Have a grown-up call your vet if your guinea pig is dull and droopy.

Handle with Care

A guinea pig does not like surprises. It does not like loud sounds or quick movements. It does not like to be grabbed.

19

Guinea pigs are fun and friendly pets.

They grunt and whistle and squeal like pigs.

They say "Wheep! Wheep!"

when they are happy.

Would a guinea pig make you happy?

Many people think guinea pigs are perfect pets.

It might be just the pet for you.

Make a Pet Care Idea Web

An idea web is a good way to help you sort information. Make an idea web about having a pet guinea pig. Copy the web below on your own sheet of paper. Use the ideas in the book to help you finish the web.

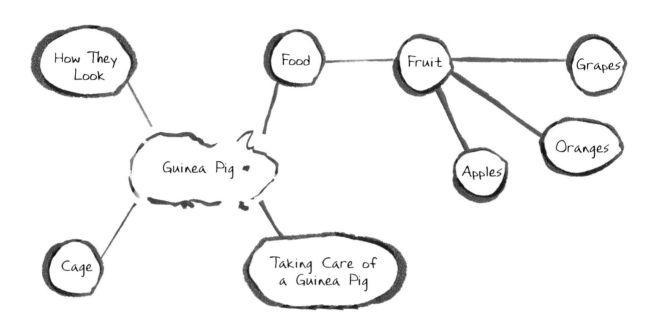

Fun Facts

- A guinea pig is also known as a cavy. (Cavy rhymes with *gravy*.)
- Guinea pigs live about six years.
- Two guinea pigs can live in one big cage.

    Two females will be good friends.

    Two males might fight.

    A male and a female can be friends, but then you will have lots of babies to find good homes for.

- A male guinea pig is called a boar.

Guide to Rodents

A guinea pig is a mammal called a rodent. The word *rodent* means "gnawing teeth." All rodents have long front teeth. These teeth never stop growing. Most rodents are small and furry with long whiskers and clawed feet.

There are lots of kinds of rodents. This chart tells you about a few of them.

Name	Fun Fact	Can It Be a Pet?
Mole rat	It lives in underground tunnels.	No
Gray squirrel	Baby squirrels are called kittens.	No
Golden hamster	It carries food in pockets inside its cheeks.	Yes
American beaver	It can use its teeth to chew through small trees.	No
Chinchilla	It rears up on its back legs and spits when it feels threatened.	Yes
Cape porcupine	Prickly quills on its back keep enemies away.	No
White mouse	It likes to live in pairs.	Yes

Words to Know

bedding—soft material for covering the bottom of a pet's cage

hay—dried field grasses

pellets—small, dry pieces of food made especially for pets

pen—a small area with a fence around it to keep animals from running away

sawdust—powdery bits of wood that have fallen off of sawed wood

vet (short for *veterinarian*)—a doctor who treats animals

23

To Learn More

At the Library

Evans, Mark. *Guinea Pigs.* (ASPCA Pet Care Guides for Kids).
New York: Dorling Kindersley, 2001.

Hughes, Sarah. *My Guinea Pig.* New York: Children's Press, 2001.

Royston, Angela. *Life Cycle of a Guinea Pig.* Des Plaines, Ill.:
Heinemann Interactive Library, 1998.

Viner, Bradley. *Guinea Pig.* Hauppauge, N.Y.: Barron's, 1999.

On the Web

ASPCA Kids' Site
http://www.animaland.org
For stories, games, and information about pets

Marty the CyberPig
http://www.cyberpig.com
For guinea pig games and information

Want to learn more about guinea pigs?
Visit FACT HOUND at *http://www.facthound.com.*